NAUGHTY LITTLE MONKEYS

by Jim Aylesworth | illustrated by Henry Cole

NAUGHTY LITTLE MONKEYS

SCHOLASTIC INC.

New York Toronto London Auckland Sydney
Mexico City New Delhi Hong Kong Buenos Aires

To all the naughty little monkeys,
who have so enriched my life,
with love!   —J.A.

To Joan, a naughty monkey if ever
there was one!   —H.C.

ISBN 0-439-68583-4

Text copyright © 2003 by Jim Aylesworth.
Illustrations copyright © 2003 by Henry Cole.
All rights reserved. Published by Scholastic Inc.,
557 Broadway, New York, NY 10012, by arrangement
with Dutton Children's Books, a member of Penguin
 Group (USA) Inc. SCHOLASTIC and associated logos
are trademarks and/or registered trademarks of
Scholastic Inc.

12 11 10 9 8 7 6 5 4 3 2 1   4 5 6 7 8 9/0

Printed in the U.S.A.   08

First Scholastic printing, October 2004

Designed by Heather Wood

Naughty little monkeys
Know a lot of tricks,
But Mom thinks they're angelic,
All naughty twenty-six.

Naughty little monkey
Has a folded **airplane**.
He flies it all around
Until the rest complain.

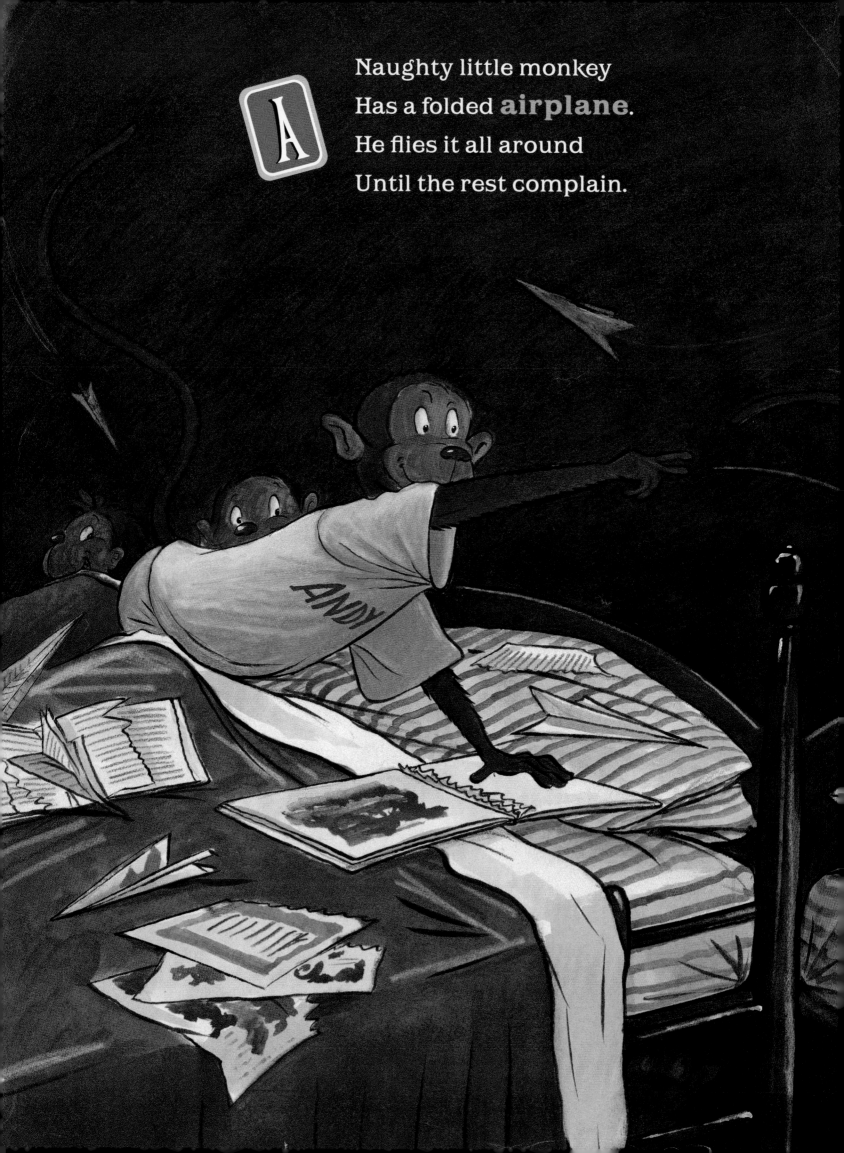

Naughty little monkey,
Jumping on her **bed**.
It won't be too much longer
Before she bonks her head.

Naughty little monkey,
Eating chocolate **cake**.
If she eats another bite,
She'll get a tummy ache.

Naughty little monkey,

Swinging on the **drape**.

The curtain rod is bending

Into a funny shape.

Naughty little monkey,
Wearing Mom's **earrings**.
She's been told before
Not to touch her things.

Naughty little monkey,
Fooling with the **fish**.
All his fingers in the bowl
Going splashy, splish, splish.

Naughty little monkey,
Playing with her gum.
Pulling pink and gooey strings
From her teeth out to her thumb.

Naughty little monkey,
Snipping off his **hair**...
But he's clipped too much now—
Off to the barber's chair!

Naughty little monkey,
He's careless with **ice cream**.
The drips are dripping down
In a steady, sticky stream.

Naughty little monkey,
She's spreading grape **jelly**.
She's got it smeared all over
Her hands and chin and belly.

Naughty little monkey,
Zooming with her **kite**.
The string is getting tangled
On everything in sight.

Naughty little monkey,
Drawing with **lipstick**.
When his mama sees this,
It will make her feel quite sick.

Naughty little monkey
Loves his baseball **mitt**.
But playing ball indoors . . .
He really ought to quit!

Naughty little monkey,
Cutting up the **news**.
If Daddy hasn't read it,
He'll surely blow his fuse.

Naughty little monkey,
Waiting by the **oven**.
When the timer starts to ding—
Watch out! There may be shoving.

Naughty little monkey,
Stacking his **pancakes**.
All the syrup's pouring off
Into brown and gluey lakes.

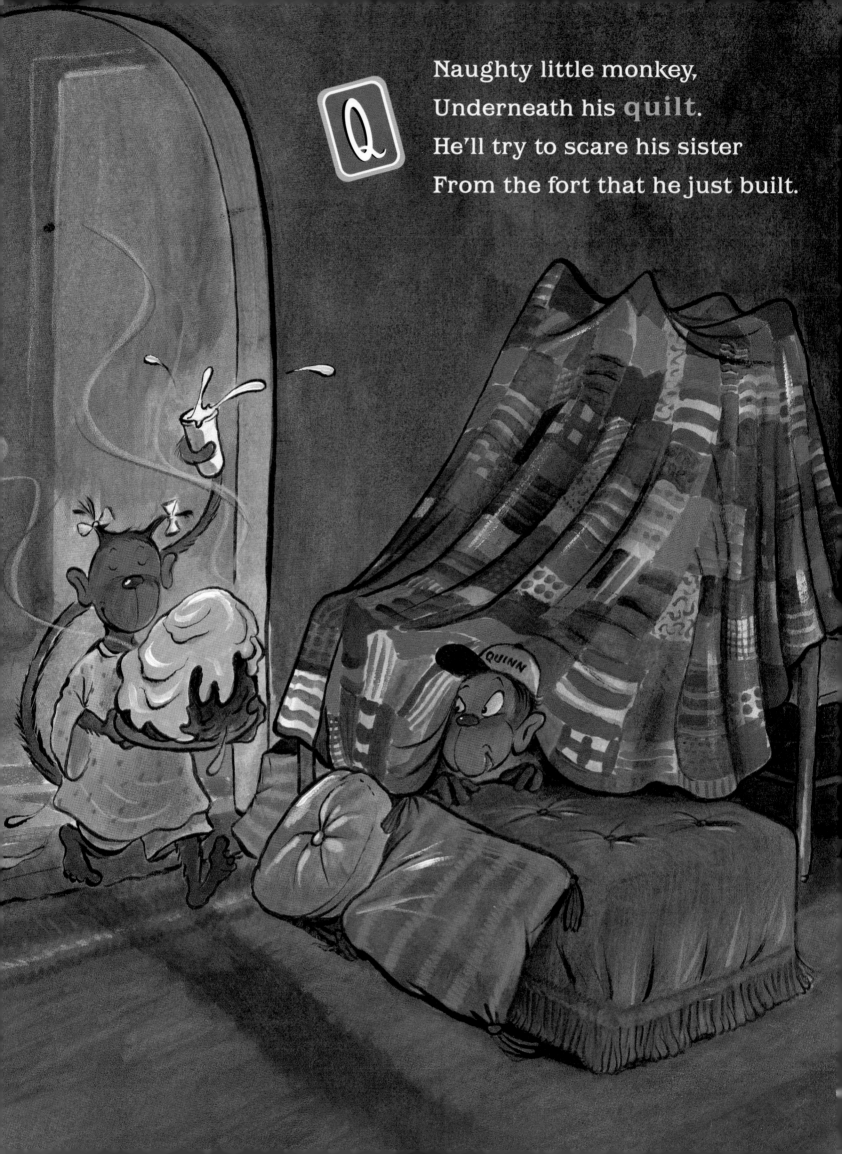

Naughty little monkey,
Underneath his quilt.
He'll try to scare his sister
From the fort that he just built.

Naughty little monkey,
Tracking up the **rug**.
Her feet are very muddy
From some holes that she has dug.

Naughty little monkey
Goes speeding down the **slide**.
She is bound to get bruised
From such a wild ride.

Naughty little monkey,
Wearing Daddy's **ties**.
He should really know by now
That such a thing's not wise.

Naughty little monkey,
Under Mom's **umbrella**.
It's far too big and heavy
For such a little fella.

Naughty little monkey,
With a brand-new **violin**.
By now her brother's patience
Is wearing very thin.

Naughty little monkey,
Splashing soapy **water**.
This way to take a bath
Her mother never taught her.

X

Naughty little monkey,
Banging his **xylophone**.
His mom and dad are wishing
That they had not come home.

y

Naughty little monkey,
Not careful with his **yo-yo**.
Watch out for that street lamp—
Oops! Now it's an oh-no!

Naughty little monkeys,

Heading for the **zoo**.

That's where all the monkeys go...

When the ABC's are through!